Harold and Harold

Harold and Harold

Budge Wilson

illustrated by Terry Roscoe

Pottersfield Press, Lawrencetown Beach
Nova Scotia   1995

Copyright Budge Wilson 1995

Canadian Cataloguing in Publication

Wilson, Budge
Harold and Harold
ISBN 0-919001-94-7
I. Roscoe, Terry. II. Title
PS8595.I5813H37 1995   jC813.'54 95-950192-4
PZ7.W45Ha 1995

Pottersfield Press gratefully acknowledges the ongoing support of the Nova Scotia Department of Education Cultural Affairs Division, The Canada Council and The Department of Canadian Heritage.

Author photo by Mary Primrose

Pottersfield Press
Lawrencetown Beach
RR 2, Porters Lake
Nova Scotia B0J 2S0

Printed in Canada

This book is for

my grandson

Lucas Alan Jarche

with love

Chapter One: Harold

Harold MacGregor was eight years old, and he lived in Nova Scotia. He had a wide mouth with a big smile. He had long skinny legs. And he had a lot of tangled curly hair which looked like a Kurly Kate pot cleaner.

Harold hated his hair. He wanted to have straight, shaggy hair, like Jason Opratko, who was staying in the summer cottage next door.

Every morning, Harold put his head under the tap and turned on the water. When his hair was soaking wet, he took his two hands and flattened it down on his head. He never stopped hoping that when he raised his arms, his hair would look exactly like Jason Opratko's. But when he took away his hands, the curls popped right up again as though they were alive.

When people — especially old ladies — met him for the first time, they would say, "My! What lovely curls!" Harold would scowl at them and say absolutely nothing. He certainly never said, "Thank you."

Harold also had a very large, broad nose. "My gosh!" his father would say. "That kid is all nose. I hope he grows into it." But that didn't bother Harold. He liked his nose. He knew that if his nose were small, the old ladies who thought his hair so pretty, might also say, "Why, you look exactly like a girl."

But Harold looked just exactly like a boy, which of course is what he was. So Harold felt very friendly towards his nose. But he didn't always feel happy about everything else.

Chapter Two: Lonesome

In the summer time, Harold and his older sister Helen, and his parents and a few aunts moved from the city of Halifax to their cottage on Squid Bay. Harold liked the cottage because it was right beside the water. He enjoyed seeing the fishing boats coming into the harbour. He loved to watch the sea breathing in and out, and to count the seagulls on the flat rocks at the edge of the bay.

But he was lonesome. All the kids in the other cottages were older than he was — even Jason Opratko, who had such nice straight hair.

Harold wished that he was nine or ten like Jason and his friends. They weren't mean to Harold. They just didn't pay any attention to him at all. They didn't seem to know he was there.

Harold couldn't even spend much time with his family because they were always busy. Helen was usually off swimming or playing Monopoly with her friends. She was four years older than Harold. Mr. Mac-Gregor only came down to the cottage on weekends, and then he'd usually disappear into the woods and fish for trout all day. The aunts and Mrs. MacGregor spent their time cooking or washing up or sitting around on deck chairs reading novels. They said they were worn out from too much work during the winter.

So Harold was almost always alone. He stood on the rocks and fed the seagulls fish heads and tails. He liked to see the birds appear as though by magic — rushing down out of the sky to fight over the food on the surface of the water. Often Harold lay flat on his stomach on the wharf and watched the sea anemones fold and unfold themselves like flowers. He looked at the crabs moving

sideways among the prickly sea urchins. And sometimes he pulled a starfish out of the water for awhile. Then he could watch its tiny feet wiggling and waving to and fro like a field of miniature wheat moving in the wind. One of the things Harold liked to do best was to jig for perch from the end of the Government Wharf. He was good at it. But it's not a lot of fun to catch a fish if there's no one to say, "Wow! That's *some* fish!"

Chapter Three : And Harold

In mid-July something special happened. One morning at six o'clock, Harold went for a walk to the Rock Bluff, not far from his cottage. He often got up early, even though his parents and aunts had a silly idea about getting extra sleep on their holidays. They woke up around nine o'clock. So Harold was all by himself.

When he reached the Bluff, there, standing stately and alone on a giant rock at the edge of the water, was a heron. The tall bird looked this way and he looked that way, but he seemed in no hurry to move. "Like me," thought Harold. "He likes just looking at things. He seems to enjoy the view."

The heron had long thin legs. "Like me," thought Harold, looking down at his bony knees.

The bird also had a long beak which took up most of the space on his face. "Like me," smiled Harold. "Except that it's a different shape. And what's more," he concluded, "he's all alone. Like me."

He watched the bird for a long, long time. Then the heron spread his enormous wings and flew effortlessly out to Ledgy Island. This was an island surrounded by ledges, where boats never landed. Harold knew that the ledges are reefs or rocks near the water's surface, where boats can be broken and wrecked when the tide is low or when the seas are rough.

Harold watched the heron disappear into the woods on Ledgy Island and said to himself, "This heron is so much like me that I'm going to call him Harold. This will be our secret. His and mine. And he will be my friend."

That's exactly what happened. Harold stopped feeding the seagulls. Instead, he took food out to the heron. Every morning, at six o'clock, he went out to the Rock Bluff

to bring Harold his breakfast. In the evening, just before sundown, he would bring the bird some supper. At first, Harold wouldn't go near the food that was brought to him. But because the other Harold was quiet and friendly, he soon stopped being afraid of him and began to eat. The tall heron was always there at six o'clock and again at eight p.m. Harold the boy talked to Harold the bird, and told him all the things he was doing and thinking — like watching the starfishes' legs and sometimes being lonesome. Harold stood very still and seemed to be listening very carefully. "A heron is a wonderful kind of friend to have," thought Harold.

And so the days passed. Even when it rained, Harold fed Harold his breakfast and supper and enjoyed a half-hour's conversation. Harold never minded when Harold spread his beautiful wings and flew off to Ledgy Island; he always knew his friend would come again.

Chapter Four : The Storm

In the first week of August, there was a terrible storm — or a wonderful storm, depending on your point of view. Fishermen hate storms because they know they can destroy lobster traps and sink boats. Sometimes, if a storm is bad enough, people even drown.

But Harold loved storms. He liked to watch all that power in the water, and to feel the wind hitting his face. He didn't tell anyone that he felt this way. He kept those thoughts to himself. Harold was full of secrets. Being lonely and loving storms were just two of the things that he kept locked up inside his head.

That morning, Harold woke up later than usual because it was so dark. It was eight o'clock. He looked out the window at the grey sky and the black boiling sea. Quickly he crept downstairs and dressed in his rain gear. The wind was so strong that he could hardly get the back door open, but after much pushing and shoving, he managed to do it.

He knew it was too windy and wild to take the shore path out to the Bluff, so he went the long way through the woods. Even there, the sound of the surf was fierce and thundering. He was sure that if he went out on the Bluff he would blow away in the wind like a flimsy piece of driftwood. So he stayed in the shelter of the trees.

From there, he could still see the large rock where he and Harold spent their secret time together. It was completely bare. In fact, it was now under water much of the time. Wave after wave crashed over the special rock; and as the tide rose, it looked as though it would disappear altogether.

Harold wasn't worried. He was just a kid, but he knew enough not to go out on the rock that day. He was certain that Harold wouldn't even consider leaving his nest on Ledgy Island to make the long trip across the raging water. He would be safe because he was a wild, wise bird, and he would know exactly what to do.

Harold stayed in the woods for almost an hour, watching the storm, and listening to the roar of the wind and waves. Then he turned around and started back to the house.

Chapter Five: The Wrong Thing To Say

As Harold was passing Jason Opratko's cottage, he could hear voices in the woods. He was so busy with his own thoughts and with the excitement of the storm that he didn't pay any attention to what was being said. There seemed to be a lot of running around and calling back and forth. Finally, through the noise of the moving trees, he caught the words, "Where's Harold?"

Without thinking, he yelled back, "He's out on Ledgy Island!"

As soon as he said it, he knew that he'd made a terrible mistake. He'd kept his secret all to himself for two weeks, and now

everyone would find out about it. Questions would be asked, and he'd have to tell them who Harold was. Then a whole lot of people would go out to visit him, and the bird wouldn't be his own special friend anymore. Worse still, they might scare Harold so much with their noise and talking, that he'd go away and never return. Or the big kids might laugh at Harold because he had a bird for a friend. He didn't think he could stand that.

Harold began to run. Maybe if they didn't find him, they'd think that someone else had spoken. Perhaps he hadn't messed up his secret after all.

When he got home, he found the house empty. Good. That meant that he wouldn't have to explain where he'd been.

It was now ten o'clock. He was wet and hungry. He left his rain gear in a heap out in the screened porch, behind the old wicker chair. Then he made himself a giant peanut butter sandwich and took it up to his bedroom to eat. From his window, the view of Squid Bay was perfect. He watched the storm for a long time and then settled down on the bed to read some comic books. But he was very tired after his exciting morning, and by eleven o'clock he was fast asleep.

Chapter Six: Missing!

Most of the neighbouring cottagers were gathered at Jason Opratko's place. They had come there to organize a search for Harold. Mr. and Mrs. MacGregor had awakened at nine o'clock to find Harold gone. Every other day he had been back at the house by eight-thirty, so of course they knew nothing about what he did before then. Not only was Harold missing on that particular morning but the terrible storm made everything scarier. His mother and his father and his aunts and his sister Helen were all wild with worry. Each of them went off to one of the other cottages to see if Harold was there.

Then all those people met at the Opratko cottage to decide what they should do next.

Mrs. MacGregor tried to keep her eyes off the angry black sea. Mr. MacGregor rushed around and asked questions about the last time anyone had seen Harold. No one seemed to have any useful information or ideas. Helen MacGregor wished she'd given him at least half of the Coffee Crisp she'd been eating the day before. Harold had asked for a bite and she'd refused. The aunts thought about all the times they'd scolded him for coming in with wet feet. Jason Opratko and his friends found themselves interested in him for the first time.

Earlier, someone from another cottage had yelled through the storm to Mr. Opratko, "Where's Harold?"

A voice had called back, "He's out on Ledgy Island!" No one knew where the voice had come from or who it belonged to.

Ledgy Island was out in the bay, visible from the cottage wharves. The children were forbidden to go close to the island, even on calm days, because of the reefs; but the boys knew that sometimes kids disobeyed the warnings and went there anyway. But to be

27

out there in this storm! Even Jason Opratko was shocked.

Mrs. MacGregor started to cry, and Mr. MacGregor patted her on the shoulder, saying, "There, there, dear. I'm sure he's perfectly safe." But the look on his face said that he didn't think Harold was perfectly safe at all. He'd noticed that a couple of the small row boats were missing, and no one knew if they'd been taken away or blown away. He tried not to think about those boats.

Chapter Seven: The Search

Mr. Opratko shut himself up in the bedroom and made a phone call. Before very long, a car arrived with two Mounties in it. A search party was formed to comb the woods and the shore path. Then a large Zodiac appeared in the bay, with three officers on board, dressed in their special suits. It heaved its way over the heavy seas in the direction of Ledgy Island although the skipper yelled out, "There's no way we can find anything in this wind!"

But Mrs. MacGregor shouted back, "Well, look, anyway! And look hard!" Then she cried some more, and Mrs. Opratko took her inside for a mug of hot cocoa.

In the meantime, many of the search party were having secret thoughts. Mr. MacGregor was thinking, "He spends so much time alone that I really don't know what he does or thinks. I should have talked to him more often. Or maybe taken him fishing with me, even though he's too young to manage fly casting."

Mrs. MacGregor was thinking, "I'm sure he'd have more sense than to go out on a sea like this. Still, you can never be sure what a kid may take it into his head to do."

Jason Opratko was thinking, "He seemed like a nice kid. Maybe we should have let him hang out with us."

Helen was thinking, "I'll never enjoy a Coffee Crisp chocolate bar again, as long as I live."

Mr. and Mrs. Opratko were thinking, "I'm glad it's not *our* child lost out there."

After a couple of hours, the big Zodiac lunged over the waves and docked at the Opratkos' wharf. When the men climbed up the ladder, they looked as wet and as weary as if they'd been out on the stormy sea all day.

"Sorry, ma'am," said one of the Mounties to Mrs MacGregor, "but there's nothing more we can do out there till the sea calms down a bit." He ran his fingers through his dripping hair and tried not to look at her face.

Then everyone went back to the MacGregors' house to try and cheer up Harold's family. The aunts made pots and pots of hot soup and coffee. Mrs. MacGregor cooked pancakes, because she said she needed to keep busy. Helen found a Coffee Crisp bar on the kitchen counter, and then she had to go lock herself in the outhouse until she stopped crying. When she came back, everyone was eating and drinking — or pretending to — and telling the Mac-Gregors that everything was going to be all right. Jason Opratko said, "I really liked that crazy curly hair he had."

"What do you mean — HAD!" shrieked Helen, and then was sorry, because three or four of the women started to cry again. Mr. MacGregor just stood at the window look-ing out at the storm, chewing on his thumbnail.

Chapter Eight: Surprise!

Upstairs in his room, Harold opened his eyes and yawned. What a noisy storm! But he wasn't hearing just a storm. He sat up straight on the bed and listened hard. Through the noise of the wind and the waves and the trees, he could pick out voices and the clatter of dishes and a lot of coming and going.

"My gosh!" he muttered, pulling on his shoes. "I'm missing a party!" He rushed downstairs.

Harold stood in the doorway of the kitchen for a full two minutes before anyone knew he was there. This gave him enough time to look around. He saw his

sister's red nose. He watched his mother mopping at her eyes while she tended the pancakes. Jason Opratko and his pals were looking miserable, sitting in front of the TV with the TV *off*. His father was pacing the floor and refusing to eat. The neighbours were whispering among themselves with brand new wrinkles on their foreheads. Finally Harold spoke.

"Some party!" he said.

He could hardly believe what happened next. His mother spilled the pancake batter on the floor and rushed over to hug him (crying), without even stopping to clean up the mess. His father was too stunned to speak, but the look on his face was wonderful to see. Helen rushed over and pressed a whole (not a half) Coffee Crisp into his hand. Jason and his pals looked as pleased as if the pitcher of the Toronto Blue Jays had just arrived. The neighbours all started talking at once, instead of whispering. But it was the aunts who really broke the ice. "Let's eat!" they announced, and everyone started laughing and talking and eating.

It was a wonderful party. He had to tell his whole story, of course, and everyone promised that if he took them to see Harold, they'd be very quiet. They would have agreed to do almost anything for him that day. He explained that he had kept on the forest path, safely away from the wind, so his parents knew that he did have a lot of sense, after all. Mr. MacGregor suggested that he call Harold "Harold Junior" just to avoid future confusion, and everyone agreed that if you left the house, you should leave a note behind, telling where you were going.

Then, the best thing of all happened. Jason Opratko came up to Harold and said, "Me and the gang are going fish-jigging tomorrow morning if the wind dies down. Wanna come? You're almost as tall as we are, so maybe you don't mind if we're older. I hear you jig real good."

The RCMP officers stayed for pancakes, and said they wished all their calls ended up like this one.

Chapter Nine: Harold and Harold

So now you know what Harold did for Harold. The rest of the summer was like a waking dream for him. He had lots of friends, lots of fun and learned to do lots of new things. He played soccer and dug for clams in the back harbour and picked blueberries and had hot dog roasts beside bonfires on the beach. His father taught him how to pitch and catch and hit softballs, and how to cast for trout.

After Harold got to know Jason and his gang really well, they didn't seem so terribly old, after all. Twin girls — exactly his age — moved into the new cottage beside the beach, and they were fun, too. Even Helen

let him play Monopoly with her friends sometimes, and they were twelve. He got to know an old fisherman and his wife who were over eighty years old, and they told him amazing stories about the long ago days when they were young. The heron didn't make every single one of those things happen for Harold, but he certainly started the ball rolling.

Even with all those adventures going on in Harold's life, he didn't forget his first friend. He still fed Harold twice a day and talked to him just as long and as often as before — although, of course, he had many more things to tell him now. He called him Harold Junior when he was at home, but when he was with him, he called him Harold. After all, that was his name.

On the last day of his holidays, Harold went out to the Bluff and had his last visit with Harold before returning to the city. He sat down on the huge rock and looked at him. He watched his handsome head turning this way and that. He admired his long legs and his tucked wings. He could feel Harold's serenity and his stillness coming right into himself, so that he felt very peaceful. When the bird rose from the rock and flew slowly off to Ledgy Island, Harold called after him, "Thank you, Harold! Have a nice winter! Goodbye!" When the heron was almost out of sight, he spoke again, very softly, "I love you, Harold," said Harold.

THE END

In 1993, Budge Wilson won the Ann Connor Brimer Award for children's literature for **Oliver's Wars**. Her books have been chosen for "Our Choice" Selections from the Canadian Children's Book Centre. She has also won the CBC Literary Competition, the Dartmouth Book Award and the Canadian Library Association YA Book Award.

Budge was born in Halifax and educated at Dalhousie University and the University of Toronto. She went on to be a columnist on child care for the **Globe and Mail**, a book illustrator and a fitness instructor. After 33 years of living in Ontario, Budge moved back to Nova Scotia to live by the sea on the South Shore.

Artist Terry Roscoe was born in Nova Scotia, graduated from Acadia University and works as a bookkeeper in Annapolis Royal. She lives in the woods with her husband, three daughters, three cats and a dog. She has also illustrated two other Budge Wilson books: **Mr. John Bertrand Nijinsky and Charlie** and **Cassandra's Driftwood**.

Other Books By Budge Wilson

The Best Worst Christmas Present Ever
A House Far From Home
Mystery Lights At Blue Harbour
Breakdown
Thirteen Never Changes
Going Bananas
Madame Belzile
   & Ramsay Hitherington-Hobbs
Lorinda's Diary
Oliver's Wars
The Leaving
Mr. John Bertrand Nijinsky and Charlie
Cassandra's Driftwood
Cordelia Clark
The Courtship
The Dandelion Garden